To Don, with love
—M. C.

For Bob & Mary Kay
—B. K.

Henry Holt and Company, LLC
Publishers since 1866
175 Fifth Avenue
New York, New York 10010
mackids.com

Library of Congress Cataloging-in-Publication Data
Cuyler, Margery.
The little school bus / Margery Cuyler ; illustrated by Bob Kolar. — First edition.
pages   cm
Summary: A happy little school bus and Driver Bob wake up early to
pick up children, drop them off at school, then head to the garage for
some minor repairs.
ISBN 978-0-8050-9435-0 (hardback)
[1. Stories in rhyme. 2. School buses—Fiction.] I. Kolar, Bob, illustrator. II. Title.
PZ8.3.C99Liw 2014   [E]—dc23   2013044353

Henry Holt books may be purchased for business or promotional use.
For information on bulk purchases, please contact Macmillan Corporate and
Premium Sales Department at (800) 221-7945 x5442 or
by e-mail at specialmarkets@macmillan.com.

First Edition—2014
The artist used Adobe Illustrator on a Macintosh computer to
create the illustrations for this book.

Printed in China by South China Printing Co. Ltd., Dongguan City,
Guangdong Province

1 3 5 7 9 10 8 6 4 2

The Little School Bus

Margery Cuyler

illustrated by Bob Kolar

Christy Ottaviano Books

Henry Holt and Company • New York

I'm a little school bus,
my driver's name is Bob.
Rumbling, shifting, clunking,
we like to do our job.

I'm a little school bus
waking up at five.
Driver Bob drinks coffee,
then we start to drive.

I'm a little school bus,
moving fast and slow,
bouncing, turning, thumping,
always on the go.

I'm a little school bus
sticking out my sign,
picking up my children
as they stand in line.

I'm a little school bus
waiting by the walk.
Boys and girls climb on,
sit and laugh and talk.

STOP

I'm a little school bus
giving Kate a ride,
letting down my platform,
so she can wheel inside.

I'm a little school bus
going 'round a bend.
"No hands out the windows,"
says Driver Bob, my friend.

I'm a little school bus
heading for my spot.
Slowing, braking, idling
in the parking lot.

I'm a little school bus
staying home today.
Snow and ice, ice and snow
keep Driver Bob away.

I'm a little school bus
turning near the guard.
Time to get a tune-up,
we pull into the yard.

I'm a little school bus,
taillight's being fixed,
creaky door's been oiled,
no more dents and nicks.

I'm a little school bus,
I jostle, thump, and sway,
picking up, dropping off,
I love my job—HOORAY!